Read-A-Rebus

Tales & Rhymes in Words & Pictures

A Random House PICTUREBACK®

Random House 🏠 *New York*

Read-A-Rebus

Tales & Rhymes in Words & Pictures

Prepared by the Bank Street College of Education
Written by William H. Hooks
Joanne Oppenheim
Betty D. Boegehold

Illustrated by Lynn Munsinger

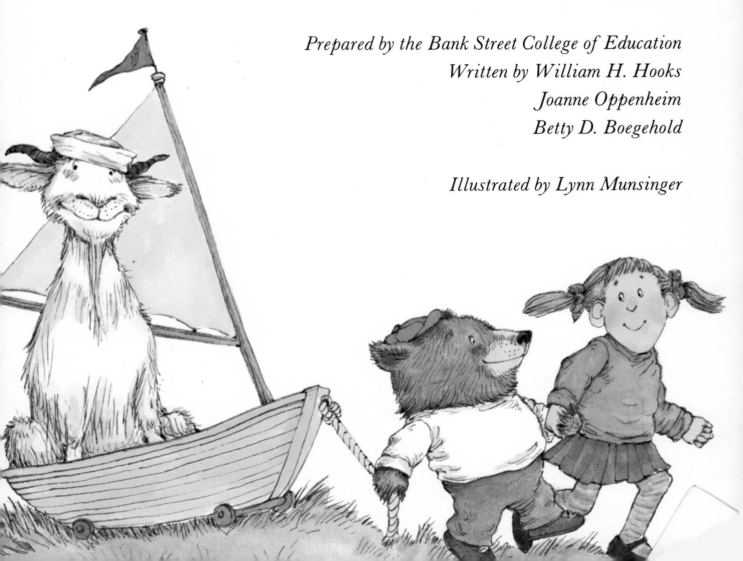

Library of Congress Cataloging-in-Publication Data: Hooks, William H. Read-a-rebus. SUMMARY: Five stories and rhymes told in rebuses introduce numbers, colors, parts of the body, and other things familiar to a child. 1. Children's literature, American. 2. Rebuses. [1. American literature—Collections. 2. Rebuses.] I. Oppenheim, Joanne. II. Boegehold, Betty Virginia Doyle.   III. Bank Street College of Education. IV. Munsinger, Lynn, ill. IV. Title. PZ5.066Re 1986 [E] 83-22282   ISBN: 0-394-85833-6 (trade); 0-394-95833-0 (lib. bdg.)

Manufactured in the United States of America   2 3 4 5 6 7 8 9 0

TO PARENTS

This book is designed for you and a young child to read together. Pictured animals and objects appear throughout the stories in place of words, and your child can participate right away in "reading" these rebuses as you read the printed words aloud.

While you read the story, move your finger under the words you are saying. This will help your child understand that we read each line from left to right and the page from top to bottom. The child will also begin to see that the little black squiggles called letters represent "talk written down." Such learning is new to the young child and basic to his or her later reading success.

The stories and poems in this book invite the child to play with rhyming and counting and to take an active role in storytelling. He or she will eagerly "read" the pictures and chant the refrains in the dialogue balloons. When your child is familiar with the book, reverse roles and let him or her have the pleasure of telling *you* the stories.

Sharing a book in a warm and satisfying way is an inviting introduction to the joys of reading. When children become active participants in the process, they're taking their first steps toward independent reading.

WILLIAM H. HOOKS
JOANNE OPPENHEIM
BETTY D. BOEGEHOLD

The Bank Street College of Education

WHAT GOES WITH ?

A and a

A  and a

A  and a

A  and a

A  and a

A and

A and a

A and

The  and the

A and a

A and a

And 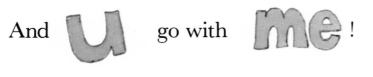 go with  !

THE BEAR FAIR

Baby Bear wanted more than anything to go to the
Big Bear Fair.

But Mama and Papa Bear always said, "You stay home
with Grandma Bear. You're too little to go to the fair."

Baby Bear always said,

It's not
fair!

Then one morning Mama Bear called, "Wake up, Baby Bear. We're going to the fair!"

Baby 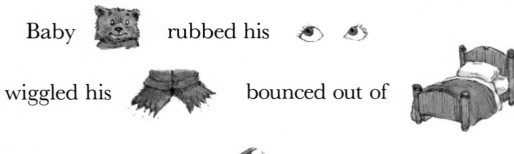 rubbed his

wiggled his bounced out of

and ran down the in his red underwear.

Baby Bear cried,  It's not fair!

Mama Bear said, "This time we're taking you with us!
Run back upstairs and put on

your blue 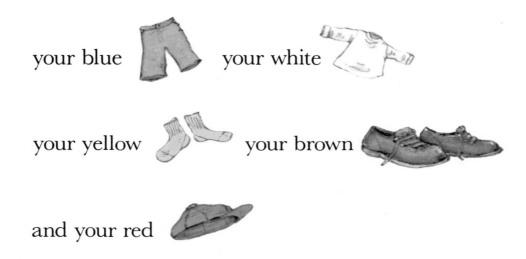 your white

your yellow your brown

and your red

And one more thing," called Mama Bear.

"Don't forget to comb your !"

So the  Bears went to the Big Bear Fair.

Baby Bear was excited to be there! But he was too little to see over the crowd of bears.

So he pulled on Papa Bear's paw and said,

It's not fair!

Papa Bear put Baby Bear on his shoulders.
"I can see everything now!" shouted Baby Bear.

Baby Bear saw...
Bears balancing on

Bears juggling yellow

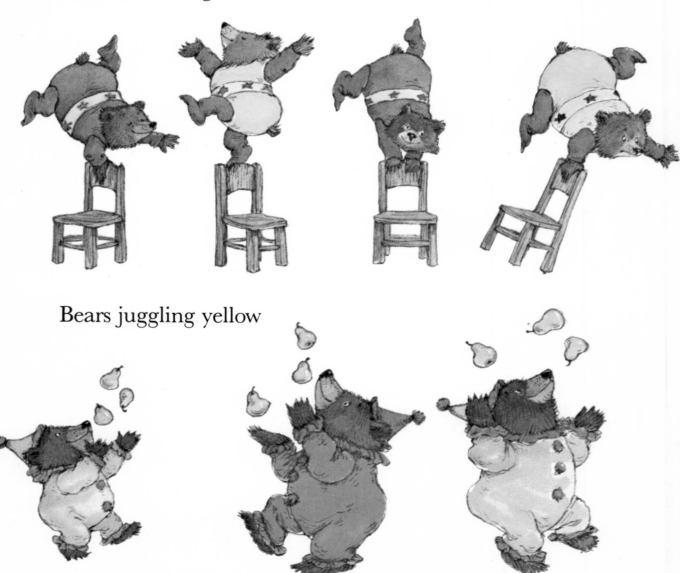

Bears floating in a

Bears flying to the

And a big white bear
Shooting through the air!

Baby Bear loved the fair.

Then Mama Bear said, "It's getting late."

Papa Bear said, "Time to go home."

Baby Bear was having fun. He didn't want to leave! He said,

It's not
fair!

Mama and Papa Bear said, "We'll come again."

So all the Bears went home.

And tucked away in his  that night, Baby Bear dreamed
of many things...

fairs and pears and a bear with !

What a
great fair!

THE PICNIC

A picnic, a picnic!
Today's the day!
From far and near
We're on our way!

Who's coming to the picnic?

 in a

 pushing

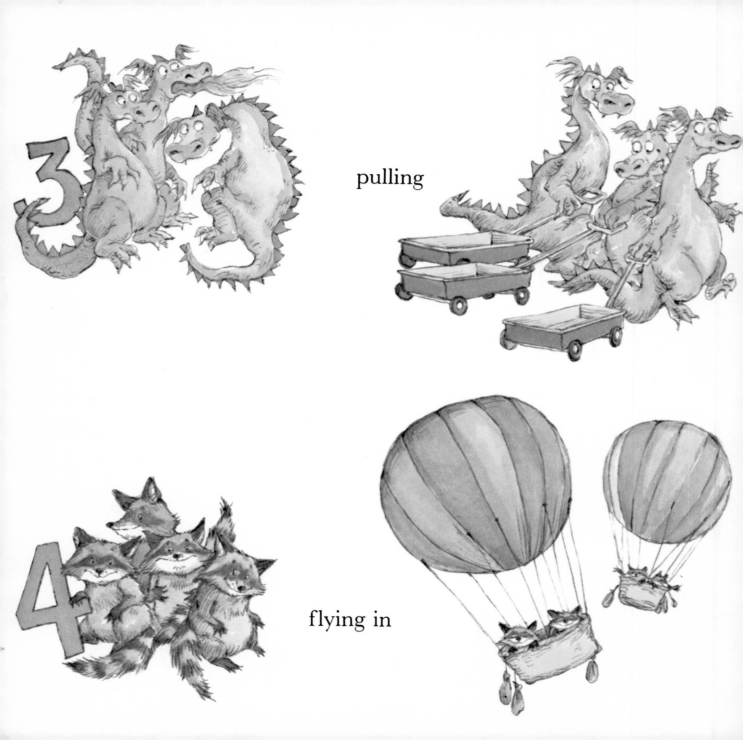

3 pulling

4 flying in

 driving

 sailing

sliding on

paddling

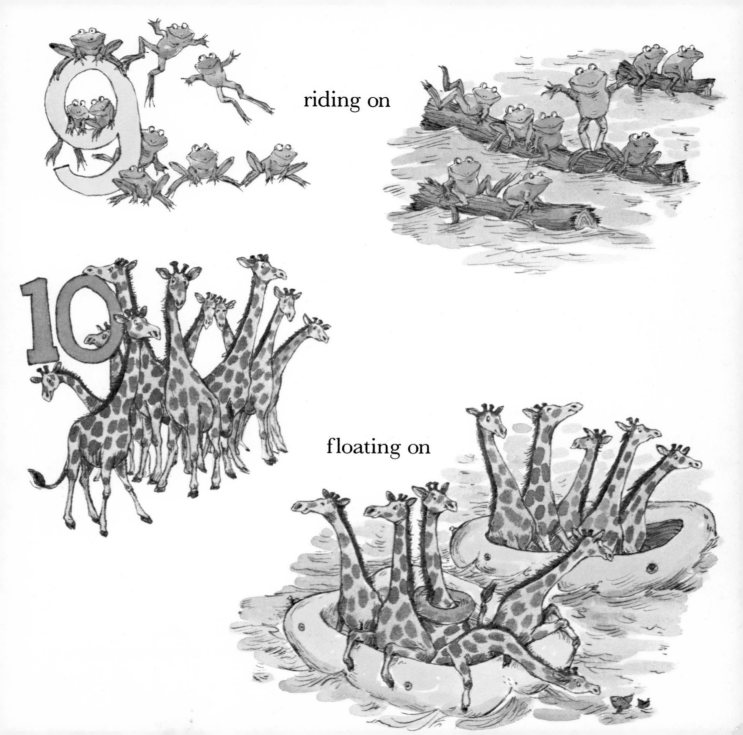

9 riding on

10 floating on

A picnic, a picnic!
Today's the day!
Everyone's here.
Hooray, hooray!

LUCY FINDS A FRIEND

Lucy had lots and lots of toys. She had

a toy

a toy

a toy

and a toy

But Lucy was very lonesome.

She had all the toys she could wish for. But what Lucy wanted most of all was a friend.

So she went out to find one.

Lucy walked along and walked along until she met a  who was holding a big fat Lucy said,

Hi, Squirrel. Will you come home with me and be my friend?

No, no!

"I must live wild and free," said the "But I'll show you where I hide my ."

The  went scamper, scamper, scamper up a  and dropped the into a secret hiding place.

"Thank you," said Lucy.

Lucy walked along and walked along until she met a  sitting in a .

No, no!

Hi, Bird. Will you come home with me and be my friend?

"I must live wild and free," said the "But I'll sing for you."

The sang and Lucy listened.

"Thank you," Lucy said with a sigh.

Lucy walked along and walked along until she met a  sitting on a  .

Hi, Frog. Will you come home with me and be my friend?

No, no!

"I must live wild and free," said the "But I'll show you how I catch a fly."

Lucy watched the go *zip!* with his tongue, and the was gone.

"Thank you," Lucy said sadly.

Lucy's eyes filled with tears. She walked along and walked

along very slowly, until she met a sitting in a .

Hi, Kitten. Will you come home with me and be my friend?

Yes! Yes!

"Oh, *thank you!*" Lucy shouted happily.

Then Lucy picked up the and ran and ran all the way home...

where Lucy and the played with

the toy  the toy

the toy  and the toy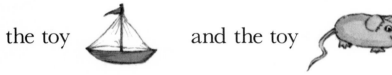

And Lucy and the were never lonesome again!

GOOD NIGHT, ME

Good night,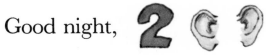

Stop sniffling,

Stay quiet,

And don't move,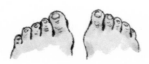

Good night, **2**

Stop fiddling around.

Good night, **2**

Time to shut down.

Good night, **2**

Sleep well, bumped

Good night, belly

Good night, all of ME.